THE TRUE STORY OF THE 3 LITTLE PIGS

BY A. WOLF

AS TOLD TO JON SCIESZKA
ILLUSTRATED BY LANE SMITH

PUFFIN BOOKS

PUFFIN BOOKS
Published by the Penguin Group
Penguin Putnam Books for Young Readers,
345 Hudson Street, New York, New York 10014, U.S.A.
Penguin Books Ltd, 27 Wrights Lane, London W8 5TZ, England
Penguin Books Australia Ltd, Ringwood, Victoria, Australia
Penguin Books Canada Ltd, 10 Alcorn Avenue, Toronto, Ontario, Canada M4V 3B2
Penguin Books (N.Z.) Ltd, 182-190 Wairau Road, Auckland 10, New Zealand
Penguin Books Ltd, Registered Offices: Harmondsworth, Middlesex, England

First published in 1989 by Viking Penguin, a division of Penguin Books USA Inc.,
Published simultaneously in Canada
Published in Puffin Books, 1996

45 46 47

Text copyright © Jon Scieszka, 1989
Illustrations copyright © Lane Smith, 1989
All rights reserved

THE LIBRARY OF CONGRESS HAS CATALOGED THE VIKING EDITION AS FOLLOWS:
Scieszka, Jon. The true story of the three little pigs
Jon Scieszka; pictures by Lane Smith
p. cm.
Summary: The wolf gives his own outlandish version of what really
happened when he tangled with the three little pigs.
ISBN 0-670-82759-2
[1. Wolves — Fiction. 2. Pigs — Fiction] I. Smith, Lane, ill. II. Title.
PZ7.S41267Tr   1989   [E] — dc20   89-8953

Puffin ISBN: 978-0-14-054451-0

Puffin Books
Manufactured in China
Set in Cheltenham Book

To Jeri and Molly

J.S. and L.S.

Everybody knows the story of the Three Little Pigs.

Or at least they think they do.

But I'll let you in on a little secret.

Nobody knows the real story,

because nobody has ever heard

my side of the story.

I'm the wolf. Alexander T. Wolf.

You can call me Al.

I don't know how this whole Big Bad Wolf thing got started,

but it's all wrong.

Maybe it's because of our diet.

Hey, it's not my fault wolves eat cute little animals like bunnies and sheep and pigs. That's just the way we are. If cheeseburgers were cute, folks would probably think you were Big and Bad, too.

But like I was saying,

the whole Big Bad Wolf thing is all wrong.

The real story is about a sneeze and a cup of sugar.

Way back in Once Upon a Time time,
I was making a birthday cake
for my dear old granny.
I had a terrible sneezing cold.
I ran out of sugar.

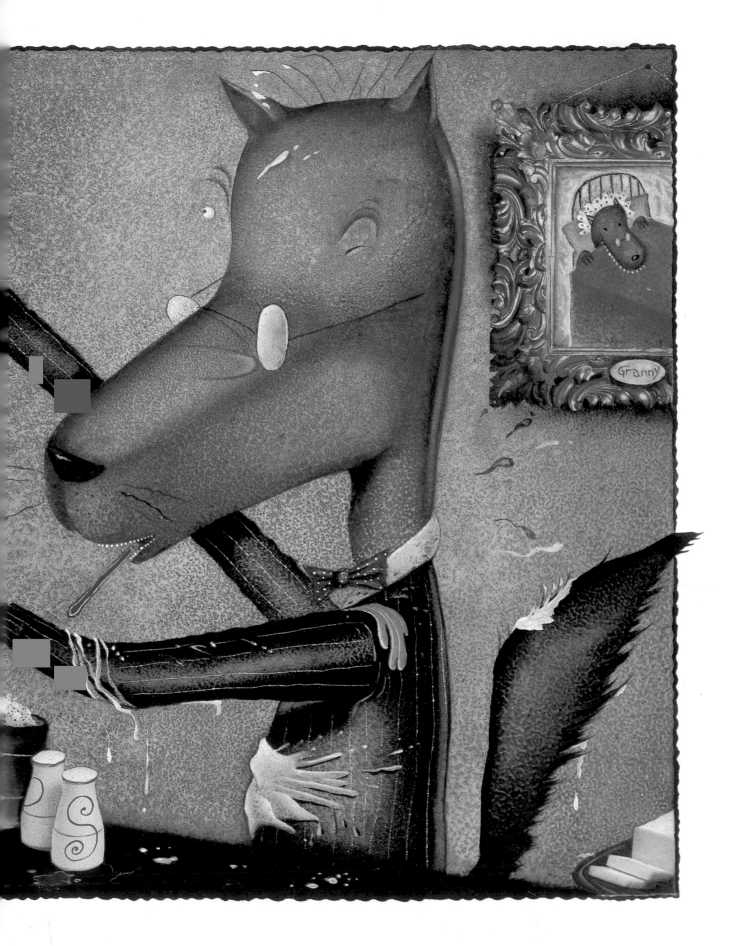

So I walked down the street to ask my neighbor for a cup of sugar. Now this neighbor was a pig.

And he wasn't too bright, either.

He had built his whole house out of straw.

Can you believe it? I mean who in his right mind would build a house of straw?

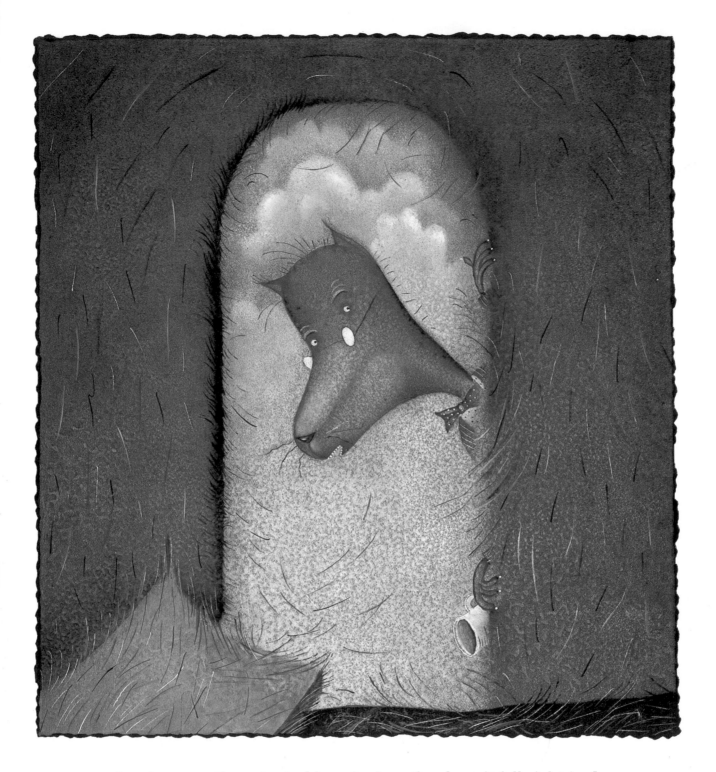

So of course the minute I knocked on the door, it fell right in. I didn't want to just walk into someone else's house. So I called, "Little Pig, Little Pig, are you in?" No answer.

I was just about to go home without the cup of sugar for my dear old granny's birthday cake.

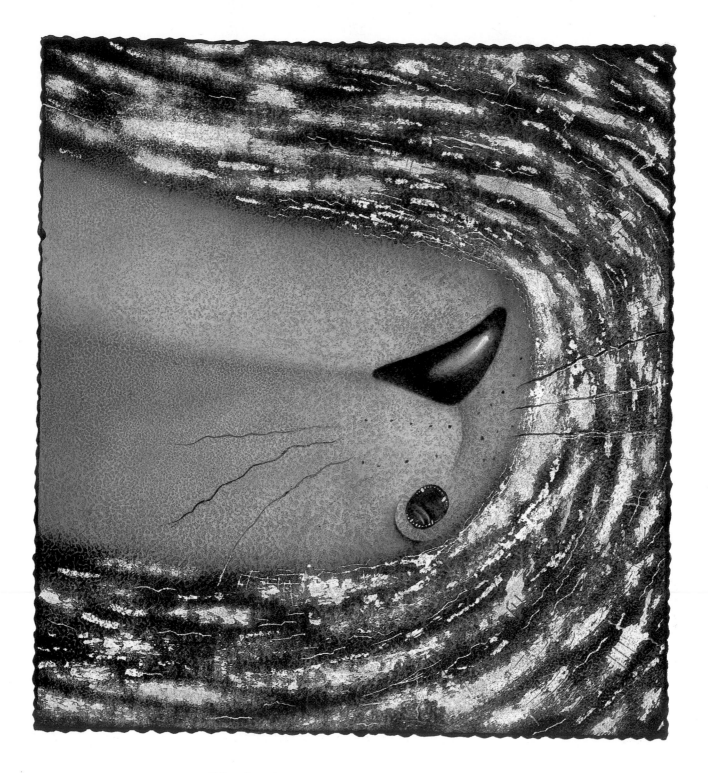

That's when my nose started to itch.

I felt a sneeze coming on.

Well I huffed.

And I snuffed.

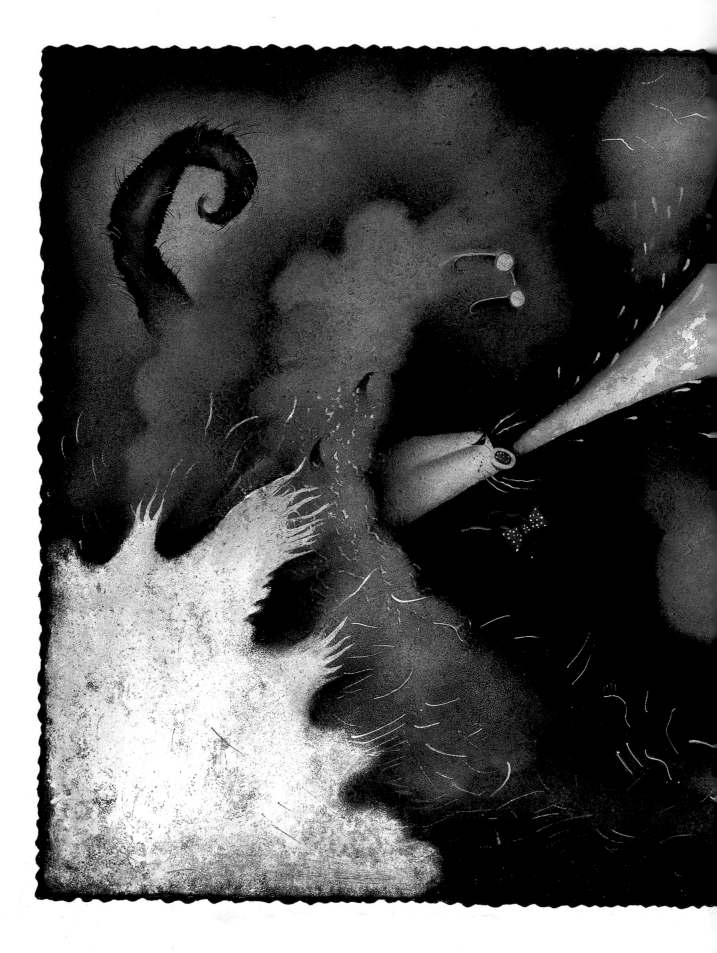

And I sneezed a great sneeze.

And you know what? That whole darn straw house fell down. And right in the middle of the pile of straw was the First Little Pig—dead as a doornail.

He had been home the whole time.

It seemed like a shame to leave a perfectly good ham dinner lying there in the straw. So I ate it up.

Think of it as a big cheeseburger just lying there.

I was feeling a little better. But I still didn't have my cup of sugar.

So I went to the next neighbor's house.

This neighbor was the First Little Pig's brother.

He was a little smarter, but not much.

He had built his house of sticks.

I rang the bell on the stick house.

Nobody answered.

I called, "Mr. Pig, Mr. Pig, are you in?"

He yelled back, "Go away wolf. You can't come in. I'm shaving the hairs on my chinny chin chin."

I had just grabbed the doorknob when I felt another sneeze coming on.

I huffed. And I snuffed. And I tried to cover my mouth, but I sneezed a great sneeze.

And you're not going to believe it, but this guy's house fell down just like his brother's.

When the dust cleared, there was the Second Little Pig—dead as a doornail. Wolf's honor.

Now you know food will spoil

if you just leave it out in the open.

So I did the only thing there was to do.

I had dinner again.

Think of it as a second helping.

I was getting awfully full.

But my cold was feeling a little better.

And I still didn't have that

cup of sugar for my dear old

granny's birthday cake.

So I went to the next house.

This guy was the

First and Second Little

Pigs' brother.

He must have been

the brains of the family.

He had built his house of bricks.

I knocked on the brick house. No answer.

I called, "Mr. Pig, Mr. Pig, are you in?"

And do you know what that rude little porker answered?

"Get out of here, Wolf. Don't bother me again."

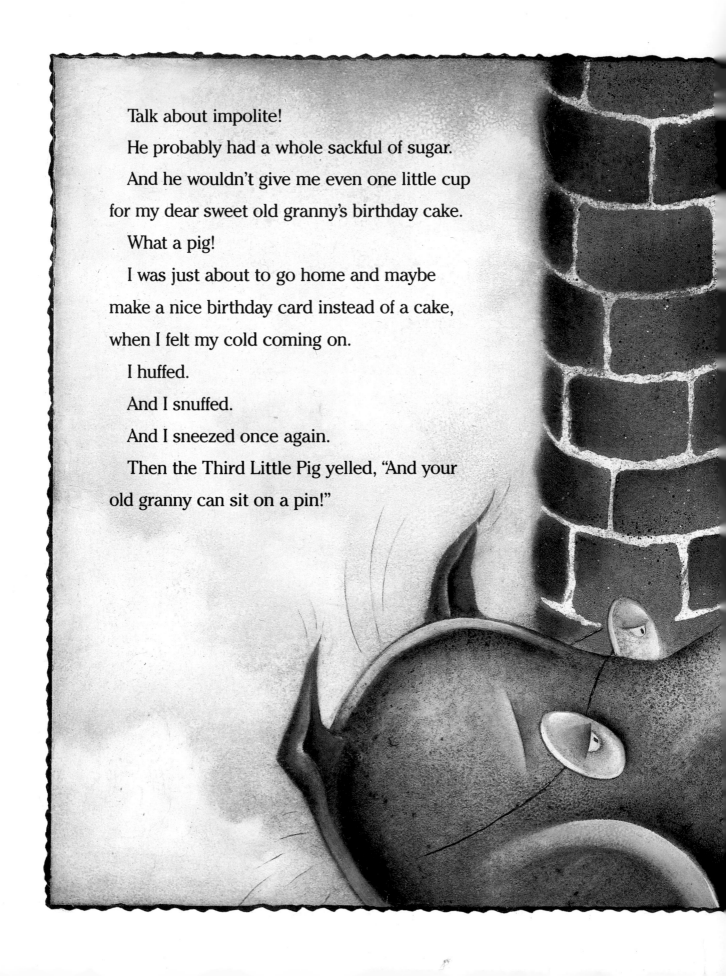

Talk about impolite!

He probably had a whole sackful of sugar.

And he wouldn't give me even one little cup
for my dear sweet old granny's birthday cake.

What a pig!

I was just about to go home and maybe
make a nice birthday card instead of a cake,
when I felt my cold coming on.

I huffed.

And I snuffed.

And I sneezed once again.

Then the Third Little Pig yelled, "And your
old granny can sit on a pin!"

Now I'm usually a pretty calm fellow. But when somebody talks about my granny like that, I go a little crazy.

When the cops drove up, of course I was trying to break down this Pig's door. And the whole time I was huffing and puffing and sneezing and making a real scene.

The rest, as they say, is history.

 he news reporters found out
about the two pigs I had for dinner.
They figured a sick guy going to
borrow a cup of sugar didn't
sound very exciting.
So they jazzed up the story with all of that
"Huff and puff and blow your house down."
And they made me the Big Bad Wolf.

That's it.
The real story. I was framed.

But maybe you could loan me a cup of sugar.